MR. SLOW

by Roger Hargreaves

Mr Slow, as you might well know, or maybe you don't, lived next door to Mr Busy.

He'd built his house himself.

Slowly.

It had taken him ten years!

And, as you might well know, or maybe you don't, Mr Slow talked in an extraordinarily slow way.

He . . . talked . . . like . . . this.

And every single thing he did was as slow as the way he talked.

For instance.

If Mr Slow was writing this book about himself, you wouldn't be able to read it yet.

He wouldn't even have got as far as this page!

For instance.

If Mr Slow was eating a currant cake for tea, it took him until bedtime.

He'd eat it crumb by crumb, currant by currant, chewing each crumb and each currant one hundred times.

For instance.

Last Christmas, it took Mr Slow until New Year's Day to open his Christmas presents.

And then it took him until Easter to write his thank-you letters!

Oh, he was a slow man.

Now, this story isn't about the time Mr Slow went on a picnic with Mr Busy.

That's another story.

No, this story is about the time Mr Slow decided to get a job.

He read all the job advertisements in the Sunday paper (which took him until Wednesday) and then he went and got himself a job reading the news on television.

Can you imagine?

It was very embarrassing!

"Good . . . evening . . .," said Mr Slow. "Here . . . is . . . the . . . nine . . . o' . . . clock . . . news."

It took him until midnight to read it!

And everybody who was watching went to sleep.

So, that job wasn't any good.

Was it?

Then, Mr Slow got himself a job as a taxi driver.

"Take me to the railway station," cried Mr Uppity, as he leapt into his taxi. "I have a train to catch at 3 o'clock!"

"Right . . . ho," said Mr Slow, and set off.

At one mile an hour!

And arrived at the station at 4 o'clock.

So, that job wasn't any good.

Was it?

And, that summer, Mr Slow got a job making ice cream. But, by the time he'd made the ice cream, it wasn't exactly the right sort of weather to be selling ice cream!

Brrr!

So, Mr Slow got himself a job making woolly scarves. But, by the time he'd finished making the scarves, it wasn't exactly the right sort of weather to be selling scarves!

Phew!

Poor Mr Slow.

He went around to ask the other Mr Men what he should do.

"Be a racing driver!" suggested Mr Silly.

Can you imagine?

No!

"Be an engine driver!" suggested Mr Funny.

Can you imagine?

No! No!

"Be a speedboat driver!" suggested Mr Tickle.

Can you imagine?

No! No! No!

But then, Mr Happy had an extremely good idea.

Most sensible.

"Be a steamroller driver," he suggested.

And today that is exactly what Mr Slow does.

Slowly backwards and slowly forwards he drives.

Up and down.

Down and up.

Ever so slowly.

The next time you see a steamroller doing that, look and see if Mr Slow is driving it.

If he is, you shout to him, "Hello, Mr Slow! Are you having a nice time?"

And he'll wave, and shout back to you.

"Yes . . . thank . . . you . . .," he'll shout.

"Good . . . bye!"

3 Great Offers for MR.MEN Fans!

3 Sixteen Beautiful Fridge Magnets – any 2 for £2.00!

inc.P&P

They're very special collector's items!
Simply tick your first and second* choices from the list below
of any 2 characters!

1st Choice
- [ ] Mr. Happy
- [ ] Mr. Lazy
- [ ] Mr. Topsy-Turvy
- [ ] Mr. Bounce
- [ ] Mr. Bump
- [ ] Mr. Small
- [ ] Mr. Snow
- [ ] Mr. Wrong

- [ ] Mr. Daydream
- [ ] Mr. Tickle
- [ ] Mr. Greedy
- [ ] Mr. Funny
- [ ] Little Miss Giggles
- [ ] Little Miss Splendid
- [ ] Little Miss Naughty
- [ ] Little Miss Sunshine

2nd Choice
- [ ] Mr. Happy
- [ ] Mr. Lazy
- [ ] Mr. Topsy-Turvy
- [ ] Mr. Bounce
- [ ] Mr. Bump
- [ ] Mr. Small
- [ ] Mr. Snow
- [ ] Mr. Wrong

- [ ] Mr. Daydream
- [ ] Mr. Tickle
- [ ] Mr. Greedy
- [ ] Mr. Funny
- [ ] Little Miss Giggles
- [ ] Little Miss Splendid
- [ ] Little Miss Naughty
- [ ] Little Miss Sunshine

*Only in case your first choice is out of stock.

TO BE COMPLETED BY AN ADULT

To apply for any of these great offers, ask an adult to complete the coupon below and send it with
the appropriate payment and tokens, if needed, to MR. MEN CLASSIC OFFER, PO BOX 715, HORSHAM RH12 5WG

- [ ] Please send _____ Mr. Men Library case(s) and/or _____ Little Miss Library case(s) at £5.99 each inc P&P
- [ ] Please send a poster and door hanger as selected overleaf. I enclose six tokens plus a 50p coin for P&P
- [ ] Please send me _____ pair(s) of Mr. Men/Little Miss fridge magnets, as selected above at £2.00 inc P&P

Fan's Name _____

Address _____

_____ **Postcode** _____

Date of Birth _____

Name of Parent/Guardian _____

Total amount enclosed £ _____

- [ ] **I enclose a cheque/postal order payable to Egmont Books Limited**
- [ ] **Please charge my MasterCard/Visa/Amex/Switch or Delta account** (delete as appropriate)

Card Number

Expiry date ___/___   **Signature** _____

Please allow 28 days for delivery. Offer is only available while stocks last. We reserve the right to change the terms
of this offer at any time and we offer a 14 day money back guarantee. This does not affect your statutory rights.
Data Protection Act: If you do not wish to receive other similar offers from us or companies we recommend, please
tick this box [ ]. Offers apply to UK only.

MR.MEN   **LITTLE MISS**
Mr. Men and Little Miss™ & ©Mrs. Roger Hargreaves

CUT ALONG DOTTED LINE AND RETURN THIS WHOLE PAGE